MARC BROWN

Arthur the Brave

"This Bionic Bunny show is so boring," D.W. groaned.

"He's amazing!" said Arthur. "I wish I could be just like him."

"Well, you're not," teased D.W.

"I'll show her!" thought Arthur. "But I need to think of something brave to do..."

"I've got it!" yelled Arthur.

"What are you doing to Mom's good towel?" asked D.W.

"Please call me Arthur the Brave," said Arthur.

"You're Arthur the Silly," D.W. giggled.

"Not funny," said Arthur.

That afternoon, Arthur took a walk.

"Bring on the bad guys!" he said. "Bring on the danger."

"Arthur, what are you doing?" asked Ms. Turner, the librarian.

"Looks like trouble," sniffed Mr. Ratburn.

"They've never seen a real super hero before," thought Arthur.

When Arthur got home, he smelled smoke.

"I'll save you!" cried Arthur.

Arthur dashed into the kitchen with a bucket of water.
He threw it on the fire.

"That was our dinner!" said Dad.

"Sorry," said Arthur.

Later on, Arthur saw Grandma Thora trying to cross the street.

"I'll help her!" he thought.

"Let me help you, Grandma," said Arthur.

"But Arthur..." said Grandma Thora.

"Don't worry," he replied. "It's safe to cross."

When they got across, Grandma Thora was not happy.

"I really didn't need to cross the street," she sighed.
"I was waiting for Mrs. Tibble in the park."

"Sorry," said Arthur.

On his way home, Arthur saw Buster and Sue Ellen.

"Help!" cried Sue Ellen. "Someone save my kitty!"

"At last!" exclaimed Arthur. "A real rescue. Stand back, everyone!"

"I'll save you, kitty," called Arthur.

Suddenly the cat jumped from the tree into Sue Ellen's arms.

"I think I'm stuck," Arthur said.

"Don't worry," said Sue Ellen. "Help is on the way."

"Hang on, Arthur!" called Binky and Buster.

Buster climbed up and untangled Arthur's cape.

"Thanks," said Arthur.

He felt like he couldn't
do anything right.

"I'll never be like the Bionic Bunny," thought Arthur that night.

Just then, he heard D.W. crying.

"Help!" she cried. "There are monsters under my bed!"

"They're in the closet too!" she yelled. "Help!"

"Turn on the light!" begged D.W. "Quick!"

"Calm down," said Arthur.

He checked everywhere.

"There are no monsters," said Arthur.

"Yes, there are!" said D.W. "Mean ones with big yellow eyes and pointy teeth and huge hairy hands!"

"I used to be afraid of monsters when I was little," said Arthur.
"Then I learned a magic spell that got rid of them."

"Will you tell me?" she asked.

"Okay," said Arthur. "Here it is:

Pat your tummy, wiggle your nose;

Tug your ears, then curl your toes.

Now say these words as loud as you can,

'I'm just as brave as I think I am!'"

D.W. said the spell three times.

"That's a pretty good spell," D.W. yawned.
"Even the Bionic Bunny could use it.
I don't think you're Arthur the Silly anymore..."

Arthur smiled and quietly tiptoed out of her room.

Back in his room, Arthur climbed into bed.

Sometimes just being a brother is even better than being a super hero.

Then Arthur the Brave fell fast asleep.